A TALE OF TWO LIONS

A TALE OF TWO LIONS

··[A NOVEL]··

ROBERTO RANSOM

TRANSLATED BY JASPER REID

W. W. NORTON & COMPANY

NEW YORK • LONDON

Illustration credits: False-title illustration by Roberto Elías Ransom; frontispiece and final-page paintings by Luis Fracchia; line drawings by Rosanna Durán.

For information about permission to reproduce selections from this book, write to Permissions, W. W. Norton & Company, Inc., 500 Fifth Avenue, New York, NY 10110

Manufacturing by Courier Westford
Book design by Judith Abbate
Production managers: Amanda Morrison and Anna Oler

Library of Congress Cataloging-in-Publication Data

Ransom, Roberto, 1960–
[Historia de dos leones. English]
A tale of two lions : a novel / Roberto Ransom ;
translated by Jasper Reid.
p. cm.
ISBN-13: 978-0-393-32936-0 (hardcover)
ISBN-10: 0-393-32936-4 (hardcover)
I. Reid, Jasper, 1959– . II. Title.
PQ7298.28.A447H513 2007
863'.64—dc22

2006029571

W. W. Norton & Company, Inc., 500 Fifth Avenue, New York, N.Y. 10110
www.wwnorton.com

W. W. Norton & Company Ltd., Castle House,
75/76 Wells Street, London W1T 3QT

1 2 3 4 5 6 7 8 9 0

To Rosa María,
Roberto Elías,
María Paula,
and Juan Marcos

On ancient maps, unknown lands were indicated by the phrase *hic sunt leones*—"here there are lions."

CONTENTS

A TALE OF TWO LIONS

·· [I] ··

CATTINO

129

Do you desire me
desire, desire
dandelion roar
of scattered seed?

OLIVER BURDEN

Rome. February 15th

My Dear Sister,

I'm writing to warn you: Cattino—the cat who is soon to
arrive at your house with my wife—is really a lion.

I gave him to Sophia a little over two years ago. I'd
seen him in a pet shop, and as it struck me that it might
be illegal to sell lions, and as I really quite liked him, I
bought him there and then with my American Express.
He took up the entire glass enclosure—no doubt meant
for Dalmatians or Irish Setters—and what I remember
best are his paws and enormous head. He was charming.
As he slept, the only discernible movement was the rise

and fall of his white belly. His markings looked like small dark horseshoes. On the attached label, instead of writing "lion cub," the veterinary zootechnician (for this is what it said on the pocket of his lab coat, although I very much doubt, given his chatter and comments, that the lab coat was his) had written "miscellaneous."

I didn't just buy him—I adopted him. Actually, I adopted *her*. We all thought the cub was female, including the veterinarian. Costanza, our cook, set us straight a few weeks later when she noticed that our feline was possessed of a certain feature. Now all that is on Sophia's mind is the question of quarantine, and while she will insist that the cub is trained, I must tell you, if she has not done so herself, that she plans to stay with you for three months. Let's see how this training holds up after three months in a Manhattan apartment! The whole notion strikes me as absurd. Madness. Folly. Sophia insists that the idea is not only sane, but sensible. She brushes aside all my objections, arguing that with Cattino at her side she'll feel safer. Besides, what are pets for? For showing off. And it had been me, after all, who had presented her, the Contessa, with this lion cub, to become the mascot for this now-not-so-young Italian couple. "Isn't he divine?" she said, gazing at him. "Too long in the limelight and you'll catch fire," I replied to the Divine One. She's taken to talking all the time about their upcoming trip, so eager that the other day I came upon her showing Cattino pictures of the Brooklyn Bridge and other New York sights. I was not included in any of this, which bothered me quite a bit, never mind the fact that we both know I can't stand to fly. I argue that Cattino is now no longer a cub, and that the Rome Zoo would be a better place for him than this house. Even if we could domesticate Cattino as they once did the camel, the camel can travel miles across the desert without water, whereas what can Cattino do? You see my point? I hope so, for your sister-in-law has now not spoken to me for a week. Is there really such a thing as a happy marriage? Or should we all be looking for the perfect pet?

The fact is, we are not doing well, not in the least. There is less between us now than even the kindness between two strangers who talk because they happen to find themselves next to each other on a bus. We annoy each other simply by being in the same room, or with a mere sneeze. I don't know what's happening to us, Anna. In all our years of marriage I have never felt this, mostly because she has always liked to hear me talk. She didn't always listen to me, but her face would turn in my direction, as if my voice were something pleasing to her. The things I said amused her, and she would laugh, and I've always felt laughter to be the best and most revealing feature of a woman. I don't mean just any kind of laughter, but the kind she revealed in our lovemaking. Mother always predicted that I'd fall in love with a woman who knew how to listen to me. It was her way of complaining that I talked too much.

Sometimes I hear Sophia say, "He's a real animal!" She says this with pleasure. Sometimes it's just her laughter I hear. Besides, the Contessa has the new and frankly terrifying habit of using the words "always" and "everything" when she speaks of Cattino.

I read in the *Encyclopaedia Britannica* that the life expectancy is likely no more than twenty-five years. I speak of Cattino here, and not my wife, given that her mother, grandmother, great-grandmother, and great-great-grandmother all lived long lives. The proof of this is a photograph of all of them together, which Sophia keeps on her dressing table. Twenty-five years! Yesterday I asked her if the love between her and this lion was truly eternal, as she often claims, in which case why must Cattino accompany us everywhere? In response, Sophia read me something about the beast from an astrological chart, with the beast sitting right there!— quite redundant, then, any talk of ascendants.

Flaws, Cattino? *Pas du tout*. As a cub, he would rub against our legs and almost always trip us over. Am I to criticize this 350-pound adolescent, question his habits, the quantity of horsemeat we have to buy to keep him fed, the sharp smell of his urine where he's chosen to mark his territory (and make no mistake—it is absolutely *his* territory), the habit he has in the mornings of jumping up on our bed and licking our faces? Sophia receives all of this in a way that makes me feel quite petty offering up these complaints. *Devour my heart* she seems to be saying to Cattino when she presses his great head to her breast. This invitation does not include me, for while Cattino is firmly lodged in my wife's heart, I occupy something more like her large intestine.

Today we were at the airport—once more confirming their travel arrangements—and also at the low point of our entire marriage. "I don't see why this is necessary," I told her. "We were so happy." In some strange way, the three of us are bound together. Ah, that eternal triangle! How do you suppose the Holy Trinity does it, gets along? It's a mystery however you look at it. But not to us! I prefer to think of them as—to quote a dear friend of mine interviewed in a rather prestigious literary review—our Father, our Mother, and Nanny Modesta.

All this has brought about a change in me so strong that I no longer take any pleasure in Cattino's company. And yet I still do not want them to arrive together in New York, at your apartment. Perhaps, in a tighter space—for your apartment, while spacious, is still when all is said and done an apartment—he will lose some of his charm and cease to appeal to Sophia. Perhaps, but I dare not risk it. I beg you, dear Anna, to do all you can to dissuade her. I promise we will visit you another time, under other circumstances.

Your brother,

Lorenzaccio

Rome. February 27th

Dear Anna,

As I have not received any response from you to my
appeals, and as the one time we did speak on the telephone you seemed amused by what I told you, I will tell
you of our parting—today I took my wife and pet to Da
Vinci Airport, and they will be with you long before this
letter—and pass on some final suggestions.

I hate to travel. You know this. I become anxious,
even when I'm not the one traveling and am just seeing
someone off. But this morning I would have done anything to be going with Sophia. I wanted to get away, as

quickly as possible, to anywhere: smoking section, seats A and B, would you prefer the window or the aisle, Sophia? In first class, of course, not so much out of any snobbishness, but rather for a certain minimum comfort. Airplanes are so uncomfortable, don't you agree? One pays to be frightened, badly fed, and forced into the fetal position for hours on end. "You and me, Sophia, we'll go together," I told her. Her response was to send me for a cappuccino and two donuts. I kept the rest to myself: We'll travel with just hand luggage—and hand in hand? Well, yes, why not?—no checking bags, traveling light— sending for whatever we need as we go—with no need for any compartments.

Compartments are like tombs, like our catacombs, and I've never liked them, ever since Mother insisted on taking us there on outings as children, rather than to the movies, or the sea, or the park, like other mothers. I like even less having to walk over them, all those small com- partments beneath one's feet. In this sense Rome is like an enormous airliner, as is any ancient city. Must we not always have something beneath our feet? I still don't like them, and the fact that it was there that San Filippo Neri received his oversized heart and his sense of humor—it did not amuse me in the least that Mother would tell us the story every single time we went. Perhaps it was also there that he was blessed with the gift of levitation, though according to Tomassi's *Lives of the Saints* he hated to do it, and, ashamed, would fall heavily to the ground, as if he had no legs, never mind wings, when they surprised him in prayer.

Perhaps Cattino would take to levitation; he'd try out his new wings and fly circles around a moon full like a saucer of milk. Airports, by contrast, are proof for the skeptics among us that purgatory does indeed exist: though not yet airborne, one sits in full view of the sky, holding tickets bearing one's name. God's mercy manifests itself amongst the standby passengers: no ticket, their names on a waiting list.

Sophia planned to send Cattino in what looked to me like a plastic coffin. She placed him in this cage, and I must confess I did not know whether to react with amusement or disbelief. Perhaps I should have been terrified. As I say, she put him in this cage so that he'd be as safe as possible while traveling. A plastic pet cage. A minor god in a cage. But she would not have him tranquilized for the flight. I would have found it humiliating, and what really enraged me was that he let it all be done to him with such evident pleasure. He displayed an almost cheerful serenity. He would approach so that my wife could stick her fingers through the bars to stroke his head and just behind his ears. They warn me that they won't fly with anything dead, and I point out the openings in the coffin which allow him to breathe.

Of course, you must be wondering how all this could be possible with a lion—even one who is not full-grown. At that point he looked just like a cat, it was a cat's cage, everyone who looked saw a cat, and the person from the airline wrote "cat" in the space where one puts the type of pet. But don't let any of that fool you.

Both my bestiary and Sophia's showed the same creature—we didn't need to imagine or invent him—but the characteristics she took note of were so different from those I had, and the description of his various "qualities"—his vices, virtues, and mysteries—varied so much from one text to the other that, even at its clearest, the word "lion" seemed fantastically ambiguous. It goes without saying that Sophia, too, collected these small zoological treatises. She is not well.

But I was telling you about the state of Cattino. I can't explain it, but it seems the reason animals don't talk is simply because they don't have to. They do, however, manage to communicate perfectly. Given our own atrophy, we read little into Cattino's behavior, but we did talk to him. Sophia would tell him not to grow, that that would be better. In this he failed completely, though he did still manage to fool our guests. When one petted him, he seemed small enough. As you know, over time, pets begin to resemble their masters, but Cattino added a twist of his own: to be able to pass either for a normal-sized cat or—less surprisingly—for a member of his true species.

He began also to imitate us—Sophia especially—like a parrot. He did not do this because he needed to learn our language: he knew from the way we would get up from our chair if we were leaving our seat just for a moment—to use the bathroom, say, or to get a sweater—in which case he would stay lying right where he was, without a flicker of his whiskers, and close his eyes again. If, however, he determined that we were about to leave the house or go to bed, he would go and fetch his leash and place it at our feet, or he'd advance along the corridor to the bedroom in order to choose the most comfortable spot, lying along the headboard on the pillows. He is a lazybones who can sleep for as much as 16 hours in a row, especially when he's had a good meal.

At first, his parrot imitation struck me as amusing, and not just me: he would sit with us at the dinner table, no need for a chair, and was the most celebrated guest at our dinner parties, even though he did not know how to use his silverware. He would wonder if for the appetizer one was supposed to use the small fork or the small spoon—he'd read somewhere that one worked one's way in from the outside.

On the way back from the airport I think I wept. I felt as if I'd lost Sophia. It's something that always crosses my mind at our leavetakings, but this time it was worse. Why, you might ask yourself, does Sophia behave in this peculiar fashion? What do we gain by asking such questions? It reminds me of one occasion: Cattino was already living with us. Sophia came to me. I didn't question the source of her excitation; in those days, I didn't ask those kinds of questions. We made love, and at one point we laughed because the cub was watching us. He always meant to take her from me. Or is it simply that I hate all cats without rhyme or reason? Capriciously? What do you think, Anna?

Your brother,

Lorenzaccio

Rome. March 12th

Anna:

Does Sophia intend to ignore me even more while she's with you in New York than when she was here with me? She swore she would write—letters, postcards, telegrams—or telephone me if she found the thought of writing too exhausting. I haven't received anything from her, and as far as I know there has been no postal or airline strike of any kind. I believe she no longer even remembers my name. She could at least come to the phone. Besides my almost-daily letters, as much as I hate to use the telephone—as you well know—I have called six different times. Sophia is all right, isn't she? She hasn't become ill? I shudder at the thought. Not to have any news of you! At least you get my letters, and I trust also that you read them. As for my calls, the only person I've actually managed to speak to is your maid. She must laugh at me, or think I'm mad. I take some comfort in knowing that you are aware of what I am suffering, but still you tell me nothing about my Sophia, apart from the fact that she is fine and does not wish to speak to me or know anything about me.

You're not secretly in with her, are you? Sometimes I feel that you are in league against me, and it doesn't help at all that I cannot picture the two of you without him. I trust he is enjoying his New York experience. No doubt you went out last night. Perhaps to a concert or to the opening of some exhibit. Then, later, dinner—both of you together, or just Sophia?—with Cattino. Alone, happy, laughing, running through the streets, leaping, yelling like adolescents, free of me, my presence, my gaze, my comments! You'd have dined regally—it's the only way Cattino knows—and I'm sure Sophia drank quite a bit. At least I'm certain that bastard will be asleep now. Thinking of them together like that makes me mad with jealousy. I would see them dead, or die myself. Never to see her again, or especially that wretch. Son of a bitch! He stole my girl! Don't hide anything from me, dear sister! I beg you to tell me everything. She's stopped loving me, hasn't she? I don't care, but tell me! Has she come to hate me so much that she prefers to torture me with silence rather than telling me the truth? I haven't been sleeping. I have nightmares. The servants tell me I shout in the night. Perhaps tonight I'll sleep better. I doubt it.

I won't put up with it! Do you know what it's like to go to the mailbox day after day, to the post office, never getting anything, any letter or note? I swear to you, with just three words—"I'm fine. —Sophia"—my entire life would change. I would know to wait for her, and to get annoyed when she decreed it. With her so far away, and not a word, I feel as if she doesn't exist, as if all my love for her is an illusion. I no longer go out. I prefer to stay here. I think I have your correct address! Have you moved? That would explain everything: the lack of response, the maid's strange behavior . . . But I know that's not it. Apart from being too convenient an answer to my problems, I've heard Sophia's voice in the background, and the sound of panting. Either I hear from you soon, or I am capable of some drastic measure.

At this moment, I don't know what this measure will be, but I will think of something.

Lorenzaccio

Rome. March 15th

Dear Sister,

Thank you for your letter. What a relief! I laughed with
such great pleasure—a great relieved hoot of joy—when
I discovered the cause of Sophia's annoyance. All
because of that! I am very sorry that Cattino never
arrived at La Guardia. That's not true. What I am really
sorry about is how hard Sophia is taking the loss of her
pet. I swear I had nothing to do with his disappearance.
Not that getting rid of him didn't cross my mind more
than once, but really I had no reason to do anything like
that. In any case, I do believe this will be good for

Sophia—but don't tell her that. Let her discover it for herself. It's better that way. The truth is—I can tell you this—that I don't mind at all what happened, and the proof of this is that I slept wonderfully last night. What Sophia says is not true: I did not tell the baggage agent to make sure the cage got left somewhere.

She used to be sure to remind me from time to time that she comes from an ancient and noble Roman family. The last time she did this, she also threw in my face the fact that there are no lions in my family's coat of arms. This is true, but I had all the lions I needed with Cattino, and more than in my coat of arms, I wanted him in the street. I would take him to the villa's front gate and let him out, to show him he was free. "Do whatever you like with your life!" I'd exclaim, with great enthusiasm. His brief, sideways glance and a certain movement of his tail were his own way of telling me that my offer held no interest for him, and he'd go back through the gate and into the house, walking right past me. Being more homebodies than true adventurers, lions prefer not to travel that much. But actually to lose a lion! Good Lord! How does one do such a thing? The agent should have told Sophia that he had cast his head into the clouds, like a poet. That he simply left the plane where he felt like it. Such privilege! Can you imagine it, Anna, him falling through the air? Or perhaps he sprouted wings. Yet another reason not to travel by airplane.

Sophia likes to fantasize. She imagines that I pressed a wad of notes on the agent and told him, "No need for any blood, just make sure he's left somewhere," lost, suspended in some unknown part of the sky that is neither Rome nor New York, as if the sun had suddenly stopped in its tracks. Or going round and round on some baggage carousel somewhere, with no one to claim him.

In fact, when I left him he seemed sluggish and wretched. According to her, my wishes were quite clear in the loud instructions I gave as they loaded Cattino on the conveyor belt: "I want my wife to arrive in New York alone."

No doubt you've noticed how cat lovers are never satisfied with having just one or two, but rather surrender their entire house to the creatures, until it looks like an occupation. They cover everything: the refrigerator, the windowsills, the couch, the rug . . . I had to be forceful, and forbid this mania in our house—can you imagine such a thing with lions?!—and Sophia's response was to fall into the dreadful vulgarity of obsession. What could be more fundamentally boring and suspect than to be a collector? Or always to want the same thing?

That whole "lord and master" business irritated me especially. This was the nickname my wife had given him. I hated to hear her talk in that way. She later added that I needn't feel jealous, since there was no comparison! With cats, there is no middle ground: one either loves them or hates them. I was the one who felt like a pet: my entire existence became a fight to get her to notice me, which I managed only occasionally, and only as a kind of stepping-stone to Cattino. Her eyes would catch themselves reflected in mine for an instant, like those of a swallow swooping to drink from a pond in mid-flight. I don't have to say that in *his* case, that same swallow would seem to have drowned. My behavior reached ridiculous extremes: I would give voice to wild thoughts, would dress in bizarre ways—coming into the bedroom at night in a swimsuit—in a vain effort to break that spell, which was for me a curse.

Thankfully, all that's over. As to the airline's explanation—it's absurd. I simply do not believe that a lion—even if he can pass for a cat—could survive for long in the cargo hold of a DC-10. Much less that he could survive unnoticed. At the time of their explanation, Cattino would have been in the air for almost 10 days. According to my own calculations, and taking into account that particular aircraft's transatlantic route, this adds up to 21 separate flights and approximately 60,000 miles, or the equivalent of 2.3 complete circumnavigations of the earth. According to the airline, the first mistake was not unloading the cage at La Guardia. The cat then got out of the cage on a flight from Frankfurt to Los Angeles. So far in his odyssey—he would by now be up to twenty-some days, and almost 100,000 miles, or seven times around the globe—he has visited three continents—Europe and North and South America— and it is thought that he has been through London, Frankfurt, Paris, Rome, Zurich, Madrid, and Nice. Sophia ought to be proud.

The explanation of the airline—that the pet would have been able to survive thanks, apparently, to the condensation that built up in the baggage compartment as the aircraft crossed various time zones and climates, and to the leftover food tossed in by baggage handlers who sensed his presence (which certainly speaks extremely well of baggage handlers: if they were able to sense the presence of a lion, the care and attention they bring to luggage must be extraordinary)—struck me as far-fetched. I've already told you about Cattino's appetite. The airline spokesman's observation—"There are many corners and hiding places in the baggage compartment where a small animal such as a cat could easily hide. This is why we haven't found him"—is 50 percent authoritative and 50 percent pure cynicism.

I wanted to send him back to the yellowed pages of some medieval bestiary. "I'm going to put you in a time machine," I'd say. One of them would be purring loudly, the other all caresses. Sophia was tinder for the flames, and my monsters' menagerie had in it just one heartbreaking lion, mouth open, roaring, a precursor of the four evangelists, beasts of the apocalypse. *They gnash their teeth at me, fix me with their withering stares, hope to devour me with those jaws* . . . And yet, when he looked at her . . .

"You're going to disfigure her face!" I cried, at the beast's near-violent licking. And to her: "Keep him away from you!"

"You're jealous," she said, laughing.

Here she was not mistaken.

"Try to resist the beast's burning spell," I insisted, again quoting the ancients, "or he'll turn everything in his path red-hot." And though it's true that all metal expands when subjected to heat, one doesn't always need the heat, I thought to myself. What Sophia loved about Cattino was that the sheikhs had hunted him, the Egyptians worshipped him, he'd adorned the thrones of cardinals, and the Catholic kings and noblemen had defined themselves by his qualities. Our mascots always celebrate us. Cattino always treated me in a much more gentlemanly way than I him. He respected the fact that I was a kind of appendage of Sophia's—unnecessary, sometimes an annoyance, but an unavoidable part of her—and his affections included me. All that was left was for both of us to fall in love with him. He would start purring as soon as he saw her. "You'll be teaching him mathematics next," I said to my spouse. But she took this as a joke. It worried me to see her walk like a lion. I looked for other feline signs or gestures in our few intimate moments together, but this proved impossible since with Cattino curled up at the foot of the bed, we were seldom alone.

Have you ever heard a lion purr, Anna? The mutual praising, quite blind, of course, of those in love, something vile and truly vulgar when it is not happening to you. Someday I'll see him paunchy and fat, I kept telling myself, to fortify my patience.

That was before his truncated trip to New York, his trip in the trunk, so to speak. Well, he will no longer be part of all that goes on in this world: not of loves, nor hates, nor jealousies. He's no better now than any dog in the street—worse: a living dog at least knows that he will die someday; a dead lion knows nothing. I suppose he's dead. Anyway, I'm not concerned about what becomes of him, only Sophia. I've always loved Sophia's navel. Her heels, too, especially the part between the bone and the arch. Did he notice how her left ear is smaller than her right? There are so many things I'd like to talk to him about, but now he's off on his second journey. His third.

His twenty-second. It's not easy to speak to one so grand. A myth.

Fabled seaman, it will all make you seasick. You'll spin around the world, never knowing whether you're east or west of the 38th meridian. You'll realize that your vessel has no vines, or seeds, or domesticated animals. You'll seek the Orient via the Occident, chase the sunrise via the sunset, rising each day again, endlessly.

Love of all loves, may you rot in your celestial coffin. May you consume the air, and may it consume you. All beings find their natural place and there fulfill their destiny. This should bring me peace. When his time came, the poor devil fell like a fiery meteor. The hole he made in the earth is no bigger than the one he put between us.

Why don't you come and visit, and persuade Sophia to come with you? It's been ages since you were in Rome. I know that Sophia will need time to recover from the loss of her pet. Please tell her that I'm ready to wait. Most likely, someone realized how much Cattino was worth, and took him. So.

Your brother,

Lorenzaccio

Rome. April 8th

Dear Sister,

Too much time has passed. I've heard nothing of Sophia.
I can no longer stand this silence. I see the lion everywhere. His only disappearance consisted in passing from
one realm to another: perhaps he shed his old physical
form and has taken on a new one. Has Sophia assimi-
lated him in such a way that Cattino is now no longer
what he was, but has become her flesh? All I can think
of in response to this awful thought is to remember a
friend of mine who had to have a big iron nail put in his
body that looked like something from the railroad. He

did not end up with any more iron in his blood. Sophia's sadness and despondency feel like an assault, like slaps to my face. Could it be that Cattino's disappearance added to his appeal?

I walk around the house certain that I'm going to bump into him, rounding a corner in the passageway, entering one of the bedrooms, going out onto the terrace, opening the bathroom door, and as that image crops up everywhere, in busts and portraits, medals, seat backs, figurines—all due to the collector's mania which seized my wife—I am constantly being startled.

I sleep on a cot on the terrace, leave the house as early as possible, and stay out all day. And yet he continues to appear, like a figure in a dream. Pliny the Elder wrote that you can tell a lion by his walk, and I find myself searching for him amongst people on the street, in advertisements . . . sometimes, I'll be looking at a face, and something in the lips, in the corners of the mouth or the spacing of the eyes will bring him back.

Why does Sophia miss him so? Why does she complain about me and curse me as she does? She doesn't even open my letters. I used to worry about Cattino's reappearance. Everywhere I went, I would see faces which *resembled human faces, and their hair was like woman's hair, and their teeth were like lions' teeth.* But the worst of my nightmares contained nothing awful in appearance. I'm with Sophia, my right arm is around her shoulders, and I say, "All right, Sophia, by all means get yourself a well-endowed pet, but remember—no carnality in this house."

Such is my anguish, my lack of sleep, my poor appetite, that I considered seeing a psychoanalyst. But as we already know from Kafka, psychoanalysis is a useless error. And so I went to see a friend of mine who is a priest. When I asked him his opinion of psychoanalysis, he claimed not to have one, and then added, a little later, with a wry smile: "It would require—wouldn't you say—quite a leap of faith?"

We talked for a time, and drank some wine, and though we spoke generally about animals and pets, I didn't mention Cattino or what had happened. My friend is of the opinion—and he assures me that many theologians share his view—that not to allow that animals might have a soul is a gross mistake. I think it was at that moment that I decided to leave. I came to feel, in the course of our discussion, that I could finally face Cattino's true whereabouts. He was right there, between us, or in me.

We all have our dark corners, that's just how it is. What good does it do to say, "I wish it weren't so?" I left there and went to the dry cleaner's to pick up a suit from which I'd asked them to remove a stain. That's it! I thought. It's one thing to remove a stain; how does one remove a lion? I have a lion inside, and I'd like it removed. The fact that they have not yet found him affords me no sense of liberation, no sense of being cleansed. His physical absence gives me little ease.

I had imagined moving forward, towards a future in which Sophia no longer required a pet. All through medieval times the lion can be found on the recumbent statues of important men. They lie on their great stone tombs. That is what will become of me, if Sophia does not come to love me again. I need your help. I refuse to let them *lock us up like lunatics, each in our own conjugal cell.* And I refuse to let the lion repose on my tomb.

··[II]··

JEREMIAH AND THE LION

For indeed we that are in this tabernacle
do groan, being burdened;
not for that we would be unclothed,
but that we would be clothed upon,
that what is mortal may be swallowed up of life.

SECOND EPISTLE OF ST. PAUL

TO THE CORINTHIANS, 5:4

I RECOGNIZED THE EYES
from my dream and knew why I'd woken up. Someone
was watching me. At first, with the sun in my eyes, I had
trouble seeing who it was. Then I realized that it was
already afternoon; the leaflets were all gone, and my pith
helmet was full of ashes. Not wanting to startle my
watcher, I kept my head resting on my crossed arms. The
man was outside in the street and I could see just his
head sticking up—like Goya's dog—just above the line of
the window. He looked at Pasha for a moment and then
disappeared.

Then I saw him again, running through the lobby.
He was dressed in feathers and necklaces, one made of

beads and one of teeth, and he dragged his dirty, wet
cloak behind him like a large tail. He smashed Pasha's
cage with his hands, shattering the glass. Two policemen
ran across the marble floor. They pulled the man away
and twisted his arm up behind his back.

One of the constables looked me over, from the tip
of my white pith helmet to the toes of my desert boots.

"Do you know anything about this?" he asked, making a gesture which took in the near-naked man, the broken glass at his feet, and the lion.

"No."

"Do you know this man?"

"I haven't the slightest idea who he is."

The near-naked man was now speaking quietly with
the watchman, who had just arrived. After exchanging a
few words of Swahili with the warrior, the watchman
informed us that he was a Masai tribesman.

"His brother was killed by a lion, and he swore
revenge."

This amused the first constable. "He picked the
right lion," he said.

"Couldn't have picked better," agreed the other.

"He's a brave one."

They laughed.

"Imagine coming here," said the first constable, "to
pick your lion."

"And dressed like that!"

They told the watchman to explain to Mr. Masai
that they were charging him with destruction of govern-
ment property.

"He'll have to accompany us."

The Masai was confused, but dignified. They seized
him before I could say anything or stop them, and took
him away, almost dragging him. I saw how they pushed
him into the van.

The watchman had disappeared, wanting no part of
the incident.

"Run!" I cried to Pasha.

But he didn't.

I left before John Redding could appear and blame
me. The broken glass was the least of it. They'll clean up
all the glass, I thought. Redding will promise Pasha a
new cage right away and have a cordon put around the
area so that tomorrow's visitors will be able to see him
without getting close enough to touch.

. . .

"SO WHAT DID YOU DO?"
Clara asked Jeremiah.

"I waited for it to get dark, slipped behind the watchman, took the lift to the basement, and went out onto the street. In all that time, Pasha hadn't moved a hair. For him to leave then, I think, would have meant running after the sun, and even though the sun was on the point of going down, Pasha had become a night creature, for whom being out in daylight was insanity. Don't be jealous, Clara, but I could have stayed there for days, just looking at him. He has the most beautiful eyes.

"Redding told me that he'd shot him right in the forehead. He would have to show off! I told him that Pasha's eyes didn't look as if they were marbles, or even jewels, but like real lion's eyes. "So they do. Fantastic!" he said. "My friend did a good job stuffing him." Do you think a hobbyist could achieve anything like that? Ridiculous. But you can't talk to Redding. A single bullet, all alone, no one to back him up, facing Pasha head-on, one chunk of metal, that's how he killed him. One shot. (Full bore.) Somehow, I doubt it. The bullet stayed in the rifle; the charge went into the air. It's the most common thing in the world now for them to bring small prey, recently killed, to the same spot over a period of weeks, each time blowing on a whistle too high-pitched for human ears. On the day of the hunt, the hired hunter leads the novice client to that spot, swearing all the time that they're in unknown territory. Standing behind the client, the guide blows the whistle, and out comes the lion like a house cat for his dish of milk. The amateur shoots from behind a blind, though he'll swear afterwards that the lion attacked him, leaping out of the bushes. That whole side of hunting depresses me terribly. And even with all that, I don't think Redding killed Pasha. I've been over Pasha's body inch by inch, and I haven't been able to find a single wound, never mind one between the eyes. Sometimes, without thinking, I'll lower one of the blinds so he won't get so much sun. Do you remember that psalm? *Many are the afflictions of the righteous, But Jehovah delivereth him out of them all; He keepeth all his bones, Not one of them is broken.* Think, Clara, a bullet which fits in my left fist. It's the same as the cage he's in now. The second follows directly from the first. It's as if they'd shot a glass cage over him! Like those fossilized insects, trapped in amber and now solid. It's awful, don't you think? Instead of a volcanic eruption, a simple rifle shot. Imagine the air around us suddenly turning solid! It must be the feeling fish have when you pull them out of the water. Or birds, when

they smash into a window. Or babies when they are
born. Once, I was looking for the wound. I sensed Pasha
looking at me. I looked back into his eyes and what I saw
terrified me. They were of a frightening beauty, all the
hues of the sun exploded in those orbits—reds, ochres,
yellows—there was a blaze of ferocious intensity around
the pupils, which were themselves the more black and
deep, each like a black sun. Do you remember that
eclipse we saw together? Those eyes held me so
absolutely that Pasha had no need of claws to make me
his prey. I was stunned, immobilized. When he released
me, he did so because that was his will; it was a completely gratuitous gesture, and then he once again
looked as if he were asleep with his eyes open, attentive
and vigilant, even with his body that relaxed. (Relaxed!
It would be more accurate to say that he looked as if he
were praying to something. Or someone. Nonetheless,
he sleeps; seeing him gives one that feeling of peace one
feels watching a child sleeping. He sleeps in the desert
of his cage, and the sands no longer have any reason to
blow. It seemed as though the Word had dried him up,
and his soul abandoned him.) I fell backwards, crying
and groaning, rolling about on the floor with my head
between my knees. When I was at last able to get up, I
clutched my stomach and felt very weak.

"I preferred, after this, to see the back of him, to walk behind him; I'd watch him as if he'd just passed."

"Aren't you thinking of going back to work?" Clara asked him after a pause. "You should at least talk to your boss."

"I don't have his number. Besides, where should I call him from?"

"You can go straight to the police station and report the incident."

"I don't think that's such a good idea. They'll blame me. There's a better chance of Pasha eating me than of their letting me continue to work there as if nothing had happened. They'll say the Masai was related to me."

"You're running away," said Clara. "That'll only make it worse. You haven't done anything."

"I'm not going anywhere. As far as they're concerned, it's my fault, and I don't want to talk about it anymore!"

"Don't shout! You'll wake your daughter. You're impossible to talk to! Think about it, and tomorrow you can go to the ministry early and explain what happened."

• • •

"I COULDN'T TELL YOU IF
his creations came out of some artistic need, or thera-
peutic, or if indeed at some point he considered selling
them. And frankly I think there have been enough questions. The whole matter is quite clear."

John Redding addressed a group of men standing
around the table in the lobby of the Ministry of Tourism.
The broken glass had been cleaned up. Redding had
gone through the desk drawers and placed the drawings
and small, handcrafted objects on the table for everyone
to see.

"Are you quite sure that Jeremiah and the Masai
weren't in some way accomplices?" Redding insisted.
"Who killed Pasha?—I did, on a safari in '82. So the
Masai had no reason to come back and kill him again.
And in any case, Jeremiah should not have fled."

"*With* the lion, according to you," said one of the
reporters.

"Exactly. I will say that they had a very unusual
relationship. Sometimes I'd come in without Jeremiah
seeing me and watch him talking to the lion or doing a
dance around him. Does that not sound like some kind

of magic, gentlemen? Something from a primitive cult? The most sensible thing would be to burn these figurines and report the disappearance to the police."

"I am a police officer," said a man dressed as a police officer.

"Very well, then," said Redding, "make a note of it."

The reporters wanted to know more. They questioned the watchman, the cleaning woman, and various other ministry staff. Jeremiah worked as an artisan or miniaturist, reproducing Pasha's image in all sorts of materials—wood, wire, paper; he always carried pliers, or a paintbrush, or a penknife, and would work as if that were what he'd actually been hired to do. The pieces themselves—or "fantasies," as he liked to call them—covered the surface of the desk, and were put away, at the end of the day, in the deepest desk drawer. He was an affable man, if somewhat eccentric. "Distracted" was the word most of his ex-colleagues used to describe him. As a collector, he categorically refused to sell any of the pieces, and would confide that each fantasy finished was another fragment of the lion's life. He never said if he thought that some finished set of the fantasies would actually give the lion back life, but his dignity in the face of what appeared to be a pas-

time born of boredom, and the fact that he would
never sign any of the fantasies—always maintaining for
himself the strictest anonymity—seemed to bestow,
according to the other employees, a very special air on
what he did.

· · ·

AT MIDDAY ON SUNDAY, there was a knock at the door and, as he opened it, Jeremiah expected to see the friendly Mr. Gavras, with a piece of liver on a white plate, whom he'd be obliged to thank for the offering, inform about Clara's and Lucy's return, and invite in, but it wasn't him. Instead, the man was a stranger who, although dressed in plain clothes, flashed what appeared to be an official police badge as he asked, "Are you Jeremiah Jones?"

"Come in, come in, please," said Jeremiah with a gesture that opened up both the door and his dressing gown. "We weren't expecting anyone. Please excuse the mess; our religion forbids us from picking anything up on a Sunday, or even changing clothes or having visitors." He laughed, to show he was joking. "Please have a seat. Let me get you some coffee."

A few minutes later, with a cup of coffee before each of them, including Clara and Lucy (who preferred a glass of milk), the sugar bowl in the middle of the table, and with various conversational topics politely tried—last Tuesday's football match, the drought, the shortage of fish—the stranger came to the point of his visit.

"Sir, I'm afraid I must inform you that you are accused of having stolen a lion," said the man, and Clara got up to pour him another cup of coffee, and to find him something sweet, a chocolate or a biscuit.

"Who is accusing me?" replied Jeremiah, hiding his glee poorly.

"John Redding, of the Ministry of Tourism. Do you know him?"

"Like a dog knows fleas."

Clara had returned, having asked Lucy to stay in her room and watch her cartoons for a while. She looked at Jeremiah with a worried expression.

"Pasha's gone," Jeremiah told her.

The only bearable thing about that job, he thought, was Pasha, and now he too was gone. The longest Jeremiah had ever lasted at a job had been six months. Six months! A lifetime! That had certainly been the record, and he doubted now that he'd ever better it, though that was always his intention in the first hours of any new job. This time he'd lasted thirty-six days. Seen optimistically: enough time for Clara to have come back to him.

"Of course, there's no proof," said the officer, ignoring Jeremiah's comment. "And I doubt you could hide a lion in this apartment!"

He made a sweeping gesture which took in the small apartment, and they all laughed.

"However, Jeremiah, you are still a suspect. All I will ask for now is that you not leave Nairobi until this matter is cleared up. You work at the Ministry of Tourism?"

"I did. I resigned some days ago."

"I tried to get him to go back," Clara interjected. "To speak to his boss."

"I didn't have his phone number," Jeremiah said, by way of explanation.

"It seems that Mr. Redding's suspicion of you is based mostly on your behavior. The minister himself won't divulge his own opinion, but he saw to it that I got a copy of a letter Redding sent him in which he makes this claim. 'It sums up,' Redding writes, 'my own opinion in this matter.' I must stress that this remains a personal letter. Nonetheless, here it is if you'd be interested in reading it."

He spread the letter out on the table so that both Jeremiah and Clara could read it, and took another sip of coffee, nibbling afterwards on a jam biscuit, and wiping the ends of his moustache on one of the paper napkins.

Your Excellency, Minister for Tourism:

I am writing you here as I fear having made an error of judgment in the contracting of Mr. Jeremiah Jones as part of the staff of the campaign to improve the public image of this honorable ministry. I would not normally write you in this seemingly rude and abrupt manner were it not for the urgency of the matter here in question. I fear that Mr. Jones is mentally ill, and that he may actually pose a danger to the lives of visitors to the Information Booth. I am in no way referring here merely to the eccentric behavior of an aging actor. This is much more than that. I hope that I am in fact mistaken in my evaluation, but I believe that he may be connected with some type of primitive cult, or—and this strikes me as perhaps worse—with some rite of black magic connected with one of the indigenous religions. Let me relate the circumstances to you so that you may judge for yourself whether or not I am exaggerating.

His behavior has always been strange, but the first time I found it alarming was when, not finding him at his usual post, I looked down and saw him sitting by the glass cage there. When I asked him what he was doing, he told me he was listening. I asked what he was listening to. "To the lion," he said, and added that if I were to listen very carefully I might also hear him. I told him to go back to his desk.

The next time, I found him standing in front of the lion. He was staring at his face. I asked him the same thing again, and he replied quite rudely that he was staring at Pasha and Pasha was staring at him! He spoke like someone in love, and you must know, Sir, what this implies.

After this, he'd keep quiet when he noticed me come in. But when he thought there was nobody about, he'd talk to the lion. He'd say: "I'm thankful that I get to live on this side." I've been a hunter for more than 30 years, and I know strange behavior when I see it. I also heard him say: "Every day I tell you about my life, Pasha. Yes, we lie . . . but everyone else lies, too." Please note here, Minister: Jeremiah lies.

Another time I came upon him dancing around the cage like a madman. While admittedly, he does this only when the two of them are alone, God knows what passersby see from the street! I do recognize the monotony and solitude of the work; I've offered him both a radio and one of those small television sets, but he's shown no interest.

I saw no more strange behavior until yesterday. Once again he was staring at the lion, but this time he was moaning, and he then rolled around on the floor, which alarmed me. I've seen too much to be shocked, but this last episode struck me as more serious than everything before put together. I'd like to avoid any possible question of embarrassment for the Ministry.

I remain, Sir, your humble servant,

John Redding
Head of Personnel

"He's an imbecile!" said Jeremiah when he'd finished reading. "They'll let any idiot file a complaint."

"Indeed."

"And they'll listen to anyone, however fantastic the accusation!"

"We aspire to be a democracy," said the officer, finishing up the last piece of biscuit. "Believe me, my dear Jones, I'd like nothing better than to leave here completely convinced of your innocence. That way I wouldn't have to inconvenience you any further. But for that I need to find out a little more about your work, all right?"

Jeremiah nodded his agreement.

"How did you meet him?"

"Pasha?"

"No, Mr. Redding!" said Clara, squeezing his arm.

"Who's Pasha?" the investigator wanted to know.

"The lion," explained Jeremiah.

"And how did he get that nickname?"

"That doesn't really matter," said Clara. "It's just a game."

"It's not a game," said Jeremiah after a moment. "You know, of course, what a pasha is? He's the chief in a pride of lions."

"Yes, but who named him this?"

Clara had gotten up from the table again, taking the empty biscuit plate.

"I did," replied Jeremiah.

"When he saw what a leader he was," added Clara from the kitchen doorway.

"Qualities no doubt evident in an animal that's been stuffed," remarked the investigator.

"Yes," said Jeremiah, without blushing. "Though it was really Redding who gave him that name, and out of arrogance. He assumed that he was the one who shot him, and between killing just any lion and killing the head of the pride . . . well, you'll appreciate the difference."

"I'd be more interested in hearing first how you got the job, and second, how you met John Redding and what you thought of him."

Jeremiah waited for his wife to sit down again, along with Lucy, who'd come back into the dining room, and for the investigator to choose a mango and peel it, before he responded. He looked at Clara while he spoke.

"I saw an advertisement in the paper. I sent in what they asked for, along with a photograph. About a week later, as I was going out into the corridor to water your plants, I tripped over a white box. It lay upright, with a note tucked into it. I hadn't expected a reply, and certainly not to be chosen like that, without an interview. I was to report for work the next Monday, at eight in the morning.

"Back in the flat, the box on my lap, the watering

can by my side, I pried apart some of the tissue paper with my thumbs, and without unwrapping the package altogether, I could make out the sleeves of a folded white shirt with a starched collar and pearl buttons. Then I saw the rest of what the box contained. I put on the outfit and faced a complete stranger in the mirror, with jodhpurs, white tunic, boots . . . I held a riding crop in one hand and a pith helmet under my right arm. I thought it was ridiculous, and doubled over in laughter. I thought you'd think it was funny.

"I ran my finger over the number and the name of the street, which had been written in a hurry, and tried to imagine the place. I let the card fall into the helmet.

"On Monday, I reported for work at eight sharp.

" 'Who are you?' asked a policeman who was standing at the entrance to the building.

" 'Sir Montgomery Abbot Lodge,' I replied, thinking he'd be amused. I also told him to get out of my way. I said this politely—'Be so good as to move aside'—though I emphasized it with a subtle movement of the imitation-rhinoceros-hair riding crop.

"He looked at my outfit and muttered that he was going to call a policeman.

" 'Another one?'

"Before he could reply, the man who had hired me appeared.

" 'Jeremiah,' he said, and the policeman smiled. 'We've been expecting you.'

" 'It's a pleasure, Jack,' I said, using his nickname to let him know I preferred 'Mr. Jones' to 'Jeremiah.'

"He was looking at me strangely. I winked at him and he tried to understand, saying that the outfit suited me very well. I ignored the insult and followed him into a building disguised as a mausoleum . . . the building, you understand; I was disguised as a big game hunter. On account of the outfit, I'd left my house before dawn. The floor was marble, cold, in black and white tiles and with a carpet of the sort they use to receive the Queen, or the Pope. The ashtrays were shaped like funeral urns, and placed like sentries along the length of the passageway leading from the street doors. Above the entrance to the other world there was a plaque with the names of the dead, and beside the names were carved their old occupations—'stockbroker,' for example—and the dates of their deaths. Or were those their office numbers? I looked up at the name of their god or high priest which crowned the passageways leading to the tombs: MITSUBISHI. A strange place for a rehearsal. I approached, trying to step only on the black squares, wondering if you would take the white ones.

"He touched me on the shoulder.

" 'You'll work here in the lobby.'

"He took me to a desk and ran his knuckles across the surface. The desk had easy access to the corridor and a good view of the glass doors which gave onto the street. A receptionist's job?

"In front of me were large windows which faced the street, and around me was a jungle of houseplants. I took one of the broad leaves and, the way you do, rubbed gently without it staining my fingers green. I sat on the desk: a smart, urban peacock. The man told me the desk had a chair and that I should use it.

"'Thank you. Very gracious.'

"'Did you say something?'

"'These plants need water.'

"'They're plastic.'

"'Ah.'

"I arranged the riding crop at my side and put on my pith helmet with its tiger-skin band. He continued to watch me. I tucked the shirt in. He smiled and handed me a pamphlet. He looked me over from top to bottom. He is an exceedingly strange person. The truth is, I couldn't imagine what it was he wanted. He didn't have the look of a director, and though there was an element of farce about the place, it wasn't a theater. 'Kiliman-jaro's Club Safari,' read the leaflet, the black letters superimposed on a flat, golden plain which stretched away towards a mountain—perhaps a volcano?—of

cobalt blue—standing alone, yet diminished neither by
its distance nor the onset of night—rising to the white of
snow which quickly became the white of the clouds. It
looked like a broken, upside-down funnel through which
the savannah poured into the sky. It seemed to be the
result of some desire of man's—no longer satisfied with
the spires of the great cathedrals, or the Pyramids—to
raise the plains up to the skies, even if in this case it
came out as just a crooked triangle. I turned the page. I
saw a picture of a man, down on one knee, holding up
what looked like a cross between the V-shaped handle-
bars of a bicycle and a pair of twisting, undulating wings,
knotted and blackened like roots just pulled from the
ground. I took a closer look, and read that these were
actually the horns and skull of a great kudu buck and a
male impala.

"'And over here,' added the man, pointing to a photograph on the left. (Yes, it was Redding; he was squat-
ting down on the banks of a lake, examining—apparently,
since his hunter's helmet shaded his eyes—the moist
earth at his feet. What could he be looking for? I
thought. It was in any case a fascinating portrait of a
wild animal.)

"'It was almost night when I found Pasha.'

"'Pasha who?' I asked, before catching on, and

then: 'Sir,' I began, handing him one of the leaflets. I finally understood what my job was to be.

"I don't remember exactly what I said.

"'Excellent!' said the man, when I stopped speaking for lack of air. 'Firm but not overbearing.'

"'You think so?'

"'You won't be alone,' he added, and gave me a half wink. I looked towards the door. 'No, no,' said my new employer, laughing. 'I'm referring to him. To Pasha. The evening finally came where *I* lay in wait for *him*.' And with this, John Redding left the two of us alone.

"At first, I could see only the plants, but then his yellow eyes gave him away. If he nodded his great head at me it was imperceptible. His half-open mouth showed off not an engaging smile of welcome but rather an impeccably straight line of white teeth. I was stopped only by my forehead bumping the glass.

"They came to see him, walking around my desk as if it were an obstacle and I another plant, stopping per-haps to knock the ash off their cigarette or drop the butt into my white pith helmet; not that I would have behaved any differently—with that hat so conspicuous on an otherwise empty table. Most of the time we were alone. When I wasn't handing out leaflets, I liked to take off my boots and socks and rub my toes on the thick carpet. I fought the urge to nap by reading the newspaper that someone always left on the desk. When I got tired of that I watched the people walk by on the pavement outside, looking for you. What wouldn't I give to see you again now? I thought, and I smoked my cheap cigarettes and talked to Pasha.

"Such was my boredom that instead of the office windows I imagined stained-glass windows depicting Pasha devouring St. Stephen. My vision continued. I swore I could hear him behind me, turned my head towards the murmur of his movements and was just able to see, for an instant, his tail rippling like a mischievous banner over the high plains, before it disappeared again. I had the feeling that Pasha was advancing, his belly low to the ground, his lithe, powerful body gliding just above the parquet. Silently, as if walking on velvet, he stalked me. When he didn't make his leap, I opened up all the desk drawers and found what was left of a pencil and some forgotten papers. I showed Pasha his portrait. It didn't seem to make any impression. I asked him if he knew of the Chimera, a distant relative of his. He hadn't had the pleasure, so I chatted to him about her for a while. He got offended by the part about the body of a goat and I didn't want to upset him any further by saying that it was better than having a body of straw. He made it clear that he had no interest in imaginary beings.

"When I woke, I thought that the desk had been turned around, or that I was somehow on the other side, since the sun was shining into my eyes. It was then I realized that it was late, and that I'd been asleep since the morning. There were no more leaflets on the table, and my helmet was full of ashes.

"'Pasha?' I murmured, but got no answer. I looked behind me and saw him in the underbrush, transformed now into pure silhouette, black against the lesser grays of the glass, now in only two dimensions, as if at night he changed again into this, and I'd have to fold him up like a map and store him in the drawer before I left for the day. I remained sitting, without moving even to breathe, and then I saw him again, as if nightfall had found him once again on the humid banks of the lake, silently watching the savannah pass from day to night. He hunched forward over his front paws to dip his rough tongue into the surface of sky and clouds, and I heard his lapping as it cast expanding circles around Kilimanjaro.

"It was then I knew that he was alive."

Clara, once Jeremiah had finished, looked at him with a funny smile. Lucy also remained sitting at the table.

"You looked after the lion?" asked the investigator.

"I looked after him or he looked after me. He was

the guardian of my dreams, that much is certain, and I, in my vigil, looked after him, though my care consisted of telling some boy not to touch the glass, or some woman not to lean against the cage. Sometimes I had the urge to grab Pasha by the tail and swing him around my head. But I never did. I never stole a lion, either."

"What else?"

"I would pull my chair into the shade beneath one of the plants and put my feet up on the desk. Sometimes I'd carve wood, trying to get his face just right. He was extremely cultivated, though he never said anything. Sometimes we preferred to nap, especially in the afternoons. We'd sleep, or he'd look off into the distance, and I'd do the same. I'd read the paper and he'd lick his paws, each of us immersed in our own thoughts. Every mind is a whole world. Often, simple gestures were all we needed. Yes, I'd know him a hundred miles away."

"Don't be ridiculous, Jeremiah," said the investigator, once he'd stopped laughing.

"I'm quite serious.

"He wasn't very expressive. His dignity didn't permit him to express his feelings and affections fully. Of course, his glass enclosure didn't help, not being much bigger than he was."

"How did he come to be here?" asked the investigator, once again becoming businesslike.

"I don't know," admitted Pasha's keeper. "One can imagine. Even if he thought to himself, I won't move a single muscle, he'd most likely end up moving it anyway, without meaning to. Many times, without being able to control it, a muscle on his back would twitch, and a small ripple would run along his body, beneath his fur, from the base of his head down to the point where his tail begins. Others didn't seem to notice it. He was tense, nervous, and exhausted. He felt lost, and confused and hungry. He fixed his gaze on me and I remained there, hanging on the expectation of that final leap, that moment when his pose would explode like a grenade, when the library lion or courthouse guardian would suddenly roar like a demon, when the dandelion would scatter on the four winds. Pasha—*leo leonis*, native of the African savannah; weight, three hundred and fifty pounds; height to shoulder, four feet three inches, as the plaque reported—was, basically, an extraordinarily fine impersonator, whose very ambiguity was at times unbearable. Those who observed him either got carried away by their own enthusiasm for him, or would just as easily vow to see him dead. Pasha simply watched them from his cage of melted sand. The thirsty shall inherit the Kingdom of Heaven. 'What is it you're waiting for?' I asked him. He wanted to be another passerby, to come through there like the others, to watch himself from outside the cage, and then to leave his immobility behind. 'What are you waiting for so intently?' I imagined a time when all that would be left would be fragments, details, constellations of glass, of sand— black, pink, and white.

"I don't know if I dreamt it. Later I thought not, even though it was the only time I saw it happen. He jumped from the glass cage with some difficulty; its small space didn't let him move in any direction except almost vertically, like a spring. I thought he wouldn't make it, that he wouldn't manage to clear it, that he'd get stuck, hanging there with his head and front paws out, his belly on the edge of the glass, and his back paws and tail still inside. I was sure the glass would break under his weight! Instead of clearing the cage, he leapt up onto the edge, paused there for an instant as if it were a fence, and then made one complete circuit around the rim of the glass, using small movements of his whiskers and tail to keep his balance, before return-ing to his usual place and pose.

"Another time, I imagined Pasha as an old and scrawny lion, excluded from the clan, alone and weak, an old Pasha whose time as head of his clan had come to an end, and who now, without the support of his lionesses, was forced to eat frogs, termites, mice, scorpions, and locusts just to survive. He stumbled, and the hyenas circled. I had no wish to see what would inevitably follow, and out of respect for my friend and his dignity, I forced myself to dissolve the vision. The hyenas would attack all at once, taking pieces of him and eating them while they still held life. But in actual fact no such thing happened. I supposed that Pasha caught rats in the building when we weren't there. Just imagine the number of rats he'd have to eat. I'd have liked to surprise him in the act, his whiskers askew and his lips a little redder than usual. His breast stained with blood. Everything pointing to his just having returned from a hunt. Imagine some Boxer dog, old and fat, caught by surprise as he crossed one of Nairobi's many parks for whatever reason. He never knew just what descended on him, or imagined that it was the vengeance of the Cats."

Jeremiah and Clara laughed.

After a prolonged silence, the investigator said, "Nonetheless, nothing you've said gives me any indication of who stole the lion."

"The lion wasn't stolen," said Jeremiah.

"Yes, I see," said the investigator. "The lion left of his own accord."

"Exactly."

"Well, as the lion went, so must I. I can't promise you anything. Jeremiah, I must ask you again to stay where I can get hold of you."

"You don't have to worry," said Jeremiah.

The officer thanked Clara and Jeremiah for their hospitality, and asked if some other Sunday they might invite him again for coffee.

"Whenever you like," they both said.

"Our house is your house," added Clara.

"With or without a lion," insisted Jeremiah.

The officer looked at him for another moment, and then smiled, slowly nodding his head, and walking backwards to make his final exit. Clara closed the door and kept silent while his footsteps on the metal stairs faded to silence.

"This time you've really dug your grave," she said. "For one reason or another, they're bound to lock you up now."

"What are you worrying about?" Jeremiah replied. "Without Pasha they can't do a thing to me. And by now, Pasha should be in the Sudan."

·· [III] ··

THE ITALIAN CIRCUS

Had I only known,
I wouldn't have come.

CHRISTOPHER COLUMBUS

THEY WOULD NEVER HAVE
accepted having a tamer—I knew this better than
anyone—not Pasha, not Cattino, their pasts being so
different and yet so alike, above all in that they were
both such kings, each in his own way, accustomed to
having people attend them, or at the very minimum
to allow them to pursue their own courses without
hindrance, one in the belly of a DC-10 and the other in
a glass cage.

The tamer disappeared, as did the tiger who had
the role of the circus wild animal, after an incident
which ended up in the papers, even though the Calavari
family, who owned the circus, did everything possible to

avoid a scandal. Some of the fault lay with the tamer, who liked to pick some of the prettiest of the little (and not so little) girls out of the audience and take them by the hand to see the beast after the show was over. That night, the niece, I believe, of the very same Don Stefano, patriarch both of the circus and of that Tuscan clan, wanted to get a closer look at the tiger, and together with a group of children—though she herself was not a child—she approached the tamer, who, as was his custom, took her gallantly by the hand to lead her there. As he had done so many times before, he opened the cage, and with the same flimsy, ridiculous leash led that fantastic creature out to face the small group of admirers nearby. The movement was so quick—Kipling would have said that the tiger was made butter by all the swift turns he made around the girl—that by the time the children had fled in terror, or been paralyzed by fright and curled up tight in knots of fear, the tiger already had his victim, the niece of Don Stefano, by the neck, and was preparing to disembowel her with his hind claws.

The tamer—for this is how we all referred to him, no first or last name, sometimes "Tiger's friend," since the routine involved just him and the one tiger from northern India, a place he'd never seen—turned out to be a brave man, which was a great surprise to me. I felt a momentary joy, as it seemed to me that in this particular case appearances and reality had briefly overlapped, and more, that in the face of this wild animal and its golden, liquid savagery, the whole grotesque sham of the tamer—theatrical, exaggerated, and vulgar—became something else altogether. Without the whip, or the chair, or roars, or forced bared fangs (the tamer had taken a file to certain of the teeth to give them an extra ferocity, and he personally saw to their cleaning), he placed himself between the tiger and Don Stefano's niece. He pried open the feline's jaws with his arms and, by kneeing him in the abdomen, succeeded in getting the tiger to release the young lady, who was taken to the emergency room at the English hospital.

The tiger seemed to turn back into himself; saddened, surprised at what had happened, he didn't know whether to attend to the children or go back into his cage. It was decided that the animal had been set off by the girl's menstruating. But it was something that had not happened in the ten years the animal had been with the circus. I know. I saw the tiger arrive for the first time, cleaned his cage, got to know his droppings, feeding, routine, the feel of his hide, all better than my own body, and it seemed to me an injustice, a great misfortune, when they decided he should die. The tamer chose to disappear the night before, thus also avoiding the pending interrogations of the police, the animal psychologists, and Don Stefano.

I believe that the girl survived; the tiger had not broken her spine, and the injuries to her neck, abdomen, and thighs turned out to be superficial . . . the tiger had teeth but no real claws. And so I looked after one less animal for quite a while, though we continued to transport and set up his cage out of habit, and it was on one of our returns to Rome that we read about the cat who had traveled 180,000 miles in the baggage compartment of an airliner. We had it on good authority that the cat was not actually a cat but a lion, young but with a mane and testicles, having heard this from one of the members of the Gibón family, also a dwarf, who works in the company which services the jets at the airport, run and staffed entirely by dwarves—many of them ex-actors and ex-circus performers—being able because of their size to get to parts of the fuselage, engines, and wings to perform the checks and repairs necessary for the proper functioning of the plane (like that film where the people and their craft are reduced to microscopic size and injected into the dying patient to travel through his veins to destroy his malignant tumor).

"Damn reporters!" exclaimed Don Stefano. "Now there's another circus. How much d'you think they paid that reporter to write 'cat' and not 'lion'? One small word. Damn them!"

So Don Stefano and his companion of the moment

and I, without a tamer, went to find out what we could of the situation firsthand, and what a mess! The lion was being held at one of the police stations, in custody like any other troublemaker, even though you could see by his face that he didn't understand what he stood accused of. There was a lady who wanted to take Cattino—this is what she called him—back to her house, no matter the cost, he was like a son to her and to the Count, who was, surprisingly, not present, even though the lady had brought along with her the chauffeur, the cook, two maids, and a gardener to back up her version of things. There was a claim against Alitalia, whose baggage manifest clearly stated a domestic cat, in a cage measuring three feet by one and a half feet by one foot high; weight: 10 pounds; cost: 20,000 lira; destination: New York; distinguishing marks: none!; additional comments: the owner, the Countess of ———, had preferred not to tranquilize the cat for the flight.

"What nerve!" Don Stefano continued his rant. "To send a grown lion like that, whose weight alone could have put the lives of the passengers and crew on that flight, 7718 to New York, in danger, throwing off all the calculations of weight, jet fuel, and balance that they have to put into the computer just before takeoff!"

All of which fell on the airline agent at check-in, who'd received the cargo that night and filled out and stamped the paperwork, and who was now also in custody, scapegoat for the world's first Latin airline, who still insisted it was a cat he'd put on board ("I've been adoring a *cat!*" the Countess mused to herself out loud), and though everyone claimed that he'd been the first and therefore the main culprit, they also had to ask themselves—based on the notion that the person who holds the cow down is just as guilty as the one who delivers the blow—how it was possible that among all the Alitalia people involved—the check-in agents, baggage handlers, maintenance staff, cleaners, catering people—no one noticed Cattino's size and weight.

The newspapers had been paid a significant amount not to print more than was necessary, and the airline had also released a convincing sum to Rome's chief of police to keep away anyone from the media over the next forty-eight hours, during which time they felt they could resolve the situation. The first mention, the only one to have appeared so far in any of the major papers, was up on the bulletin board. Don Stefano had gone over to read it, and I was a few inches behind him, so that I could hear his comments. The press had treated him very badly at the beginning of his circus career, something he would never forgive.

"Damn journalists! You don't often see outfits as corrupt as *U.S. News & World Report*, UPI, Reuters, Xinhua. I know these reporters have to get ahead, but look how they use the story as a threat. The reporter's name—Ed Lyons—is the only true thing in the whole text. Then immediately the lies start. First comes the gender change. Of course the agency would be American! Shameless mercenaries! See how they make everything into a soap opera? Nation of wanderers, globe-trotting tourists, they make the lion's misadventure sound like a pleasure tour of the world's continents and major capitals of Europe! That's all that's left—in the future you won't even get off the plane! Seven times around the world! Next they'll be sending kitty-cat to Venus on one of NASA's shuttles. 'Kitty Visits Venus!' Have you ever heard such nonsense?"

We were there inside the police station because to get in, you needed to give the guards at the door a password, and the password was: "We're from the circus." The place seemed like a circus, too, all the more so when the Countess began to yell:

"Cattino! Cattino! D'you see him? Didn't I tell you? Oh, my Cheshire cat, must you smile and disappear? This is all a terrible misunderstanding! A grotesque frame-up!"

We turned towards where the noble lady was pointing, and there behind the bars we saw a small cat. No one there—police, security guards, attorneys,

politicians, circus people—was the type to be easily
impressed, but what we saw threw everyone into a
silence which only grew deeper, as the small unfortu-
nate creature once again took on the size and appearance of a full-grown lion.

"Ah, the child is father to the man!" exclaimed Don
Stefano "Fantastic! It's a prodigious freak of nature! It's a
double! It's a ghost that not even Doctor Angelicus himself would have dared dream up!"

All of this was said very quietly, so that only I could
hear. The last thing the principal shareholder and patriarch of the Italian Circus wanted was to put his enthusiasm on display, so he let everyone else continue with
their discussions, which had taken a new turn and
become more intense since the brief spectacle offered by
Cattino, who was watching the ruckus from his cage as
if it were a bad television drama, giving lie to the con-
cerns his ex-mistress had expressed, nearly shouting
(though apart from this she seemed quite refined) about
the ill effects of imprisonment on her gentle, sweet pet.

The suggestion was made to put him down, though
in whispers, and avoiding the gaze of the condemned,
during a moment in which the Countess had stepped
out into the passageway for a Coca-Cola, but the animal's mysterious power inspired a general feeling of fear,
a respect, a superstitious and primitive attitude, unspo-

ken but quite clear in the suggestion which immediately followed and was unanimously approved: to place Cattino in a zoo, preferably Rome's, where it had always been the tradition to accept just about anything from lions, from one mischief to the next, this latest mischief being preferable, and there being, in any case, hardly any Christians left, let alone martyrs.

"The zoo?" asked the Countess. "Are you insane? Do you know the life Cattino is used to? He'd be better off as a Paris cabbie!"

The police chief had finally managed to get hold of the zoo's director, the veterinarian Maglio.

"Quiet! Let me speak! Yes, exactly. One moment he's a lion and the next he's a cat. Yes, I know. No, I'm talking about a house cat. No, no, he's not an Angora. I'm quite serious, Director, he looks like any other stray cat. No, I don't think it's a good idea to release him into the Trevi Fountain." Here the police chief covers the mouthpiece and looks at us. "He wants to know if we've thoroughly weighed and palpated the animal and listened to his chest." Now, again resuming his conversation with the director: "I think that's an excellent suggestion—if we want to learn anything, the best thing to do is to palpate him. You wouldn't like to come and palpate him yourself? Please don't take offense, Director. I only refer to your qualifications as a man of science."

Turning once again to us, as he replaces the receiver: "He hung up on me. Would one of you be so good as to carry out Director Maglio's recommendations?"

The Countess was willing to oblige, but the police chief said that though he regretted it deeply, Madame Countess was really too emotionally involved for her observations to count for anything. Don Stefano grabbed me by the knee. "Later," he said in my ear, "you'll be able to touch the animal. Once Cattino is with us."

To send him to some African game reserve, to another zoo, to the faculty of Veterinary Medicine, to release him by night in the Villa Borghese park, or in St. Peter's Square, any of these would be cause for a scandal which would be too costly or simply too much trouble. The most plausible thing was to send him to Nairobi, and from there to a game reserve, though someone there would surely notice his distinctive qualities before setting him loose.

"You want to return him to the jungle?" asked the Countess.

"Strictly speaking, Madame, lions don't live in the jungle," said one of the lawyers, somewhere between flirtatious and pedantic.

"I know that, you fool!" replied the Countess. "You know what I mean! What do you suppose Cattino would do in a place like that? He doesn't know any other lions.

He'd speak Italian to the gazelles. You want to exchange statues, columns, verandas, and terraces for cassia trees. Cattino is accustomed to living in a garden. Don't try to tell me that there's no difference between Kenya and a villa in Rome, except for the garden being English instead of Italian!"

"Madame Countess," interjected the police chief, "we can't continue to let Cattino live as a pet in your villa. I'd like nothing better than to indulge you this whim . . . but I simply can't. You know this." Here he indicated the letter on his desk, bearing the Count's letterhead. "I fear that all in all it would have been preferable to have the cat keep flying around the globe—or at least the Rome–Frankfurt–New York part of it—for the rest of his life. I don't understand how he managed to survive." Here he laughed, shaking his head. "I imagine you saw the article in today's paper, saying that he managed supposedly by licking the condensation which formed as water drops on the ceiling of the baggage compartment, and eating the scraps of food that the baggage handlers left for him, as well, perhaps, as some mice and any other creature who might have inhabited these jets, as in times past the cockroaches, fleas, and rats, separately or feeding on each other, would infest the old galleons—I personally have seen men fast, days, sometimes even weeks, almost always political activists or human-rights workers; only yesterday I was leafing through a magazine which had something about a technique used by the yogis to remain buried alive for days at a time, or completely still, hardly breathing, their pulse almost stopped; but a lion!"

During the police chief's impassioned speech, Don Stefano whispered in my ear that he was sure the lion must have eaten some of the leather suitcases in the baggage compartment. "You've seen how those bags arrive at the airport. Or perhaps it's the baggage handlers who, handling so much luggage that travels to places that they can't hope to, simply become wild. There isn't a survival story worth its salt in which someone doesn't end up eating a suitcase, or at least a shoe."

"I'm afraid I see no solution here," concluded the police chief.

"I do," said Don Stefano.

He approached and occupied the chair beside the desk, dispatching as he did so a young police lieutenant with a small gesture of his hand, directly in front of the police chief. Then, in another gesture, slow, ceremonious, and magnanimous, with a great elegance and majesty, he proffered his card to the chief. The police chief received it, touching it with only the tips of his fingers, as if handling an extremely delicate object, and read: 'Don Stefano Calavari. The Italian Circus.'

"Is this a joke?"

"Not at all," replied the great circus leader, and he once again commanded the room through his presence and gestures, as he directed himself to the Countess: "And I assure you, noble lady, that Cattino will be a happy lion—" here he chuckled, "and cat—with us. He can continue his human friendships, you'll be able to visit him when and as often as you like, he'll have the arrangement he's become used to—needless to say, no tamer will be involved; I'll sign an agreement with you in which I'll pledge to look after him for the rest of his natural life."

"Or until he dies of boredom," said the Countess.

Don Stefano continued, "He'll travel. He'll see the world. He won't live in a five-star hotel, but he will be part of the best circus in Europe; he won't want for excitement. I know it won't be the same as living with you in your lovely villa, Countess, and I'm sorry about that . . . I don't wish to seem vulgar, but as a demonstration of my suitability, and of the life that awaits Cattino with us, I'd like to offer some assistance in order to help conclude this affair satisfactorily for all concerned.

He seemed to be asking the Countess for Cattino's hand, and there was something decidedly provincial and Old World about the whole scene, but Don Stefano was the first person the Countess had paid attention to in the whole time we'd been at the police station. From beneath his cape—he was eccentric in a most traditional way: his costume was a pure copy of a music-hall magician, though his thick hair and hands added a different aspect—he pulled bundle after bundle of blue lira banknotes—it looked like millions of lira—and stacked them on the desk, using a trick favored by our illusionist to make the piles appear to be even larger than they actually were.

Do you really think a cat like that would ever accept having a tamer? He'd come out into the ring when it was his turn and sit himself in front of the audience. Then, with an expression of the greatest possible boredom on his face, he'd switch from lion to cat and back to lion just as he must have gone from Rome to Frankfurt to New York. The audience, not surprisingly, didn't believe what it was seeing, and Cattino was the most popular act of every show.

As if that wasn't enough, one day he started speaking to the audience in Italian! *Cattino, caro, chi è il tuo primo amore? Ma dai bimbo. Chi ti vuole bene.* It was like a Beginning Italian class. It caused great hilarity, that rough and raspy voice saying those things. The laughter was followed by even greater wonder. It was, one had to admit, quite affecting to see Cattino sitting alone on the platform in the empty ring, only a few feet from the front row of the audience.

Occasionally a spectator would rush towards the front, intending to enter the ring and unmask Cattino, but they'd never make it past the low barrier, just a couple of feet high, which separated the audience from the ring, for at that short distance, you could see that while Cattino might be an enigma, he was also without doubt a lion, enigma or not. Usually our intrepid spectator would remain at the foot of the barrier, or sitting on it, amazed but not wanting to look like a coward.

Bimbo, bambino, bella creatura de dio. I cannot tell you how many times I witnessed that, and it impressed me easily as much every time. I cleaned his cage, changed his water, served his meals, I found him the occasional lioness, I called for him when it was his turn in the ring, and I'd appear for him again when the ringmaster signaled to me, but a tamer?—not a chance. Before Cattino appeared, I had never gone into the ring in front of the crowd. Of course, I became very fond of him.

I don't think it needs to be said that he was a great charmer.

. . .

RIGHT, THAT'S CATTINO;
what can you tell me about the other lion?

Pasha appeared while we were on tour in Nairobi.
One morning I found him with Cattino in his cage and
at first I thought Cattino had learned to duplicate himself. I saw the newcomer before he could see me, thanks
to the way the path leading to the cage let you glimpse
ahead through the crates of props, costumes, and luggage long before you got up to the open space around it,
and in this way I could also see that he was alive and
that he moved very naturally, seeming to enjoy Cattino's
company. But as I got up close to them, the new lion
became absolutely still, paralyzed, and in the half hour I
spent trying—I didn't want him to feel frightened or set
upon—I wasn't able to get any reaction.

I returned later with Don Stefano, telling him on
the way what had happened that morning. When we got
to the tent he was able to see what I'd seen: from a distance, the two lions frolicking like cubs, but up close, on
making that last turn and appearing in front of them, the
new one once again turned stiff and became apparently

lifeless, as if he were stuffed. Don Stefano all but wet himself in his excitement. He grabbed his crotch giddily and yelled, "Oh, my dear, dear lions!" He ordered me to make sure that the new lion, who for the time being we'd simply call "Lion," would not leave the way he'd arrived. He would see to fixing the paperwork to show that Lion had belonged to the Italian Circus for a long time, in case anyone should think of claiming him. Did he come directly from the savannah? our great circus leader asked himself. Or did he just fall from the sky? It's July. Perhaps his constellation fell to earth in a shower of stars.

He sent for a locksmith (meaning that I went to fetch him) who installed a double padlock on the cage and asked me why we had a live lion and a dead lion together in the same cage. I made a gesture to indicate that they'd been a pair. "Ah, a couple!" he said, with evident sadness, but then, after watching them a while longer, he asked, in a very knowing voice, "Husband and wife, eh? And both of them with a mane!"

Lion was younger than Cattino, and wilder, with an energy which at times had him running crazily back and forth in his cage, or tormenting Cattino, gnawing at him or giving him light pats with his paws until he got a reaction. But he looked up to him, there was a hierarchy in that tiny clan, and Cattino was the chief, which suited him well, with his restraint, refined manners, indifferent air, and greater age.

Don Stefano, who emerged as a white hunter during our long and oddly successful stay in Nairobi—I have always been put off by this part of him, coarse and phony—frequented the smarter hotel bars and recounted his exploits, though it was never clear to me whether it was the lions or his audience which were the game. The extent of his great conquests usually consisted of catching some small prize and bringing it back to the circus to prepare on an open fire and share generously with us, though he'd set aside the best parts, fresh and raw, organs and innards, for Cattino and Lion, who he was always trying to win over.

The hard thing was getting Lion to relax. With time, and our daily interactions, Lion came to accept me, but only me: he kept up his old ways in front of anyone else, including Don Stefano. I'd wait until Cattino had almost finished speaking in Italian, then I'd lead Lion into the ring, a colored scarf covering his eyes, talking to him softly all the time to prevent him from stiffening up. Once I'd led him to where I wanted him, at the same height as Cattino but on the opposite side of the ring, I'd remove the scarf and instantly—I would check that neither his pulse nor his breathing changed—he'd freeze. The audience would see him walk in and then freeze completely, and there was no way to explain away what they'd seen as an optical illusion, or a switch, or any kind of trick. Most of them accepted what they saw with a kind of silent respect. With time, once I was surer of Lion's trust, I invited members of the audience to come down into the ring to touch him. When they'd gone back to their seats, I'd replace the scarf, murmur gently to him, and lead him back out.

He was christened one night by a member of the audience. I didn't invite him, in fact I hadn't asked any-one down when a rather skinny man with graying hair jumped into the ring and went over to stand in front of Lion. "Pasha! Look at Pasha!" he said, in a voice which was at once solemn and moved. At first I thought he was drunk, or perhaps slow. But the lion moved the tip of his tail as if he knew him. He had a little girl of about six in his arms, and was leading by the hand a woman some years his junior, who seemed reluctant to follow him.

When he had finished talking, he put the girl down and they began to dance around the animal. They were a strange family, not only because of the differences in age and race. You could tell that the wife had agreed to come to the circus for the girl's sake, and that she had never expected her husband to behave like this, and now regretted her decision. She seemed to treat him with the tender resignation of those who love a rogue too much.

Jeremiah, as the woman called him, again brought his daughter closer so that she could rest her head on the lion's heart; he had noticed that it was beating.

The name stuck. The circus's clowns had fun with Pasha. Their latest game, cooked up while we were in Mexico City, was to bring the lion into the middle of the ring on a wheeled platform, eyes uncovered so that he'd be completely stiff. As they wheeled him in, he'd seem to be in a trance. The clowns, dressed as movers, would busy themselves with the apparently stuffed lion. One of them would take a set of instructions out of his pocket and read them, and then they would all try to lift the lion, grabbing at his head, his paws, his middle.

"Jesus! He's a heavy bastard!" said the shorter of the two.

"I bet they forgot to take out his guts," said the other.

"And he stinks!"

"Like a lion!"

The audience loved this charade, thinking that the lion actually didn't weigh very much.

"Christ, he's alive!" said the other.

The short one suggested that they go back to the van—they'd hauled everything you could imagine from one end of the capital to the other, even beyond, but they'd never had to deal with a lion—and just say they'd lost the order.

"Did you see that?" said the other one.

"What?" The short one surveyed the crowd, searching.

"He moved!"

"Sure, look how much he weighs. He's just settling, like the Cathedral, or the Palace of Fine Arts. Or, better, like the National Palace! Anything here that isn't cracked, it's settling."

"I'm serious."

"So am I. Hang around long enough and you'll even see it crap. It's full of shit. Just like you. Let's go. It's time to eat."

The audience was as skeptical as the short clown, since Pasha hadn't moved.

The other one kept it up, suddenly jumping back: "Did you see that?"

"Let's go. I'm starved."

"But he moved, Gus!"

"Sure, sure," he agreed, condescendingly. "Whatever you say." The audience laughed, pitying the other mover. "It wasn't the lion that moved, it was the image of the lion."

"What? Knock it off, Gus!"

"It was his ghost that shifted."

"You think it's still with him? I don't think so, Gus. I think his soul is somewhere else now."

"Animals don't have souls; you should know that, you're educated. Remember—we live in the city!"

"Did you see that, Gus? His fur moved like he'd had an electric shock!"

"Really?" replied the short one, a little annoyed now, as Pasha looked exactly the same.

"His whiskers moved!"

"Really?"

"He looked at me!"

"Real-ly?"

"His tongue peeked out!"

They'd improvise in this way, until finally the short one would grab his companion by the shoulders and pull him away from the lion: "Don't think about it. The whole thing is in your head."

Once the movers had left, and were presumably in their van and on their way to some other part of the city, I'd wrap the scarf around Pasha's eyes, and, to the astonishment, the exclamations, and the applause of the audience, I'd lead Pasha out of the ring. The act had many variations. Sometimes, we'd start the act with my leading Pasha in on a leash. I'd take the scarf

off him in the middle of the ring and he'd freeze. I'd
move off to the side, and wait with the audience for the
arrival of the clown movers. The crowd loved this;
they'd drive themselves crazy knowing all along that the
lion was alive.

· · ·

WHAT HAPPENED THAT EVENING?

What we should have expected. Pasha and Cattino had left their cage three nights earlier. It was the last time I saw them. I don't think I left the cage unlocked. This was not the first time they'd gone off, and at first we weren't particularly worried, since they didn't usually go far or seem to have much interest in anything that went on outside of the circus, though Don Stefano would always worry when we lost them.

When they hadn't come back the next morning, Don Stefano ordered the circus closed and the announcement made that we did not yet know our next tour stop. What he really wanted was to give himself time to find the lions before it got out that they'd disappeared. It always greatly worried the circus man that his stars might be stolen, though he justified this, claiming that they couldn't give a performance that didn't include the lions, since that was what people mostly came to see, and in this he was right.

He came into my trailer on the point of tears, and asked me to organize the search. All I could think of was to assemble everyone from the circus and have them comb Azcapotzalco, the neighborhood we were in, starting close to the circus site and then spreading out in a widening circle. Everyone got a map, a flashlight—since we were starting the search at night—and a canvas sack. On receiving these last items, they cursed me, especially the dwarves. I explained that the sacks were for trapping any strays they came across, and I showed them how to throw the material over an animal to trap it in the bag. It was better not to ask openly about the lions, but rather to keep their ears open and strike up conversations with people who might be able to tell them something, though this would prove difficult, as very few of them spoke Spanish. Those were the instructions, and they all looked back at me with faces that showed they hadn't understood a word, cursing me softly in their mother tongues.

Don Stefano stayed in his trailer, imagining the worst—that someone had stolen his only real treasure. They were the ones who made the show, who filled the seats. He moaned, saying he'd willingly trade the entire Gibón family—who were extraordinary clowns—or the trapeze artists—one of whom, painfully well-endowed, was his lover—and so on, for the lions.

Twenty-four hours later the circus was full of cats, though none of them was Cattino, and the circus people

refused to go out again, as some of them had suffered
various humiliations the last time, not to mention the
two who were missing, who had last been seen being
flung by police into the trunk of a squad car.

I sent another group of the braver ones out across
the city, dressed as photographers. Their mission was to
bring me information on any figure, image, or statue of a
lion, for which they would have to get close enough, one
way or another—and I suggested a few—to confirm that
the animal in question was alive. If it was Pasha, up to
his usual tricks, they were to ask him where to find Cattino, and then all come back together to the Italian Circus. They returned with pictures of several live lions,
taken in the zoos and at another circus; and of several
dead lions, taken in a particularly bohemian boutique in
the Zona Rosa, in various restaurants where jungle animals were part of the décor, in the house of some people
from the tony Las Lomas neighborhood; but not one of
them was Pasha. I knew that one would not be far from
the other.

I got hold of maps of the capital and of the metro-
politan areas of the State of Mexico, having decided that
Pasha and Cattino had entered the sewer system or the
Metro. I considered dressing up as a supervisor and
going to inspect progress on the works at shaft number
five, but when I learned that beneath the city there were

6,000 miles of storm drains and that more than 75 miles of these were almost 800 feet deep, I decided to try something different, something which would not take me so far from the surface. Let others keep bringing water to the city, only to discard it again, I thought. Let others try to control the floods. Impossible, in those two systems of thousands of miles of tunnels and pipes, in that subterranean labyrinth, to even hope to find them.

But then that night I went to talk to the men who do the maintenance on the Metro tunnels between one and five in the morning, and though they told me several tales of marvelous creatures in the tunnels, they were mostly either prehistoric or heavy metal in flavor. I didn't want to say, "You haven't, by any chance, seen a lion, or maybe two?" for I was afraid that someone would reply, "Now that you mention it . . ."

Don Stefano spent the entire next day searching the Metro system, from when it opened until it shut down for the night, from one end of the city to the other, leaning out to peer into the tunnels, and several times some charitable soul pulled him back from the edge of the platform, thinking he was about to jump. "It's not that bad," one told him.

The other day, he conferred with both his chief banker and chief lawyer, to see if it was a good time to sell a circus. He confessed to me that he'd considered selling without admitting that Pasha and Cattino were no longer a part of the Calavari family. We would never find them.

I thought of leaving, of renouncing my life in the circus. But I want to say this: the lions were not the only ones I took care of. There are a lot of other animals. As an example, I look after eight elephants, one of which was born just this spring. And while you may think lions are such wonderful creatures, elephants have nothing to learn from them. They work when they're supposed to, and in their off time they fall in love, play pranks, revel in their baths, gossip. Another time we'll speak of them instead.

That night we heard a report that one lion had been killed and another injured near the Military Academy on the Cuernavaca Road. Can you imagine: to have crossed the entire city over three days without having been spotted? Don Stefano and I took a taxi. They'd found both of them under a bridge. Pasha was dead. "And the other lion?" we asked. They told us there wasn't another lion, but that there'd been one lion and one cat (Cattino!) and that the lion had looked like a statue. That proved it was them.

"A cat?" we asked in unison.

"Yes," said the police lieutenant. "The officer who fired insists that when he fired he saw a lion. The vet from the zoo gave us the right dose for a lion, not a cat. He was there, too."

"And the lion?" asked Don Stefano in a quavering voice.

"It's a cat," stressed the lieutenant, and he brought out a canvas bag and emptied it onto the desk. We all stood looking at the body of a stray cat. That's not Cattino, I thought, and knew that Don Stefano was thinking the same thing.

"An overdose," said the lieutenant.

At that moment, another official entered the room.

"That's not the other animal they killed under the bridge," said the man, showing a certain annoyance with the lieutenant and smiling at us.

Don Stefano whispered to me that even with Cattino alone, the Italian Circus could survive. I thought of Pasha, and felt very sad. They drove us to the zoo in a patrol car, with the lights flashing and the siren going. There, standing at the cage, we saw him. He was alone, and he was a male lion, but he wasn't Cattino. He was older, though he had the same markings, or very similar.

"Is it him?" Don Stefano asked me. His anxiety was not relieved.

"I don't know," I said.

"They've stolen him!" moaned Don Stefano. "The bastards have stolen Cattino!"

I asked if I could stay alone with the lion. I told Don Stefano that I would come back to the circus and find him later that night. I got no response. At first the animal looked at me, but then he ignored me. "Are you Cattino?" I asked him. He didn't answer me, but I can't say for sure that it wasn't him. Something had changed, and if it was in fact the same lion, I doubted that he'd go back to his old life. As I left the zoo, I didn't know what to think. The only thing I was sure of at that moment was that I had no desire to go back there, to the Italian Circus.